Eli and Mort's Epic Adventures
Colorado Summer Road Trip

About this project

The idea for Eli and Mort's Epic Adventures Series stems from the joy we experienced watching our kids ski, snowboard, bike, hike and have the time of their lives growing up in the mountains. We wanted to share that joy and the beauty of Colorado with the world. We decided to write a series of books through the eyes of a child on an epic adventure -- a series of books for adventuring kids like you! This is the ninth book in the Series, "Eli and Mort's Epic Adventures Colorado Summer Road Trip."

When considering the concept we imagined what a child might see and feel when they stood at the top of the mountain, and thought, 'Who better qualified to illustrate the book than the children that live here'? As a result, we agreed that the background illustrations should be drawn by children from Colorado.

About the characters

Eli, a 5-year-old boy, and his pal Mort the Moose are the best of friends exploring the world together. When others are around Mort is a stuffed moose but to Eli, Mort is his best friend and partner in fun. In this book, they are experiencing all that the summer in Colorado has to offer.

Eli and Mort are dedicated to the loves of our lives,
Josh, Heath & Will.

Created by Elyssa and Ken Nager
Written by Elyssa Nager
Graphic design by Ken Nager
Published by Resort Books Ltd.
Background illustrations by the children of Colorado
Character Illustrations by Eduardo Paj

Printed in China
September 2020

Thank you

We love our friends in Colorado. Mort and I think you are AWESOME! Special thanks to Eduardo Paj for making us look so good.

Thank you to Meaghan Walsh and Elise Meier, the art teachers at Willow Creek Elementary School and Crested Butte Community School respectively for inspiring their children to submit their drawings.

"A big hooray!" for all of the AWESOME children who submitted their illustrations and their parents for their support.

Visit **eliandmort.com** to order our latest adventure, check out our events or to just say, "Hi!"

The Illustrators

Eli and Mort would like to thank the AMAZING local children, ages 6 to 17, that illustrated the backgrounds! Below are some of their favorite things to do during the summer in Colorado. What's yours?

Paddle Board, Grand Lake

Ava Moore
Willow Creek Elementary School
9 years old
Favorite: Swimming

Breckenridge

Jake Dierenbach
Willow Creek Elementary School
10 years old
Favorite: Camping

Colorado Sunset

Bella Volkman
Willow Creek Elementary School
10 years old
Favorite: Swimming

Woodward at Copper Mountain

Heath Nager
Eagle Valley Middle School
14 years old
Favorite: Friends, Soccer and Skateboarding

Welcome to Colorado

Eva Thomas
Vail Mountain School
16 years old
Favorite: Hiking

Hot Air Balloon, Steamboat

Lindsay Cook
Boulder High School
14 years old
Favorite: Climbing 14ers

Alpine Coaster, Vail

Imogene Martinez
Brush Creek Elementary School
6 years old
Favorite: Taking Martinez adventures

Flatirons, Boulder

Eric Kim
Willow Creek Elementary School
11 years old
Favorite: Swimming

Downhill, Winter Park

Tyler Abbott
Gypsum Creek Middle School
12 years old
Favorite: Playing sports, riding bikes

Eagle

Gage Stowell
Eagle Valley Middle School
11 years old
Favorite: Mountain biking

Fort Fun, Fort Collins

Emma Crosbie
Willow Creek Elementary School
11 years old
Favorite: Hiking, biking, paddle boarding

Rodeo

Tula Baker
Brush Creek Elementary School
10 years old
Favorite: Camping

Colorado National Monument, Grand Junction

Montana Palmer
Eagle Valley High School
14 years old
Favorite: Singing

Rocky Mountain National Park, Estes Park

Hannah Popish
Aspen High School
16 years old
Favorite: Paddle boarding

Lake Dillon

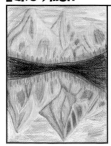

Cate Counselman
Vail Mountain School
13 years old
Favorite: Hiking

Hot Springs

Sidney Shapiro
Willow Creek Elementary School
9 years old
Favorite: Glenwood Hot Springs

HorseBack Riding, Aspen

Ana Jaramaz
Aspen
Elementary School
7 years old
Favorite: Hiking,
eating ice cream

Camping

Oliver Ropp
Willow Creek
Elementary School
9 years old
Favorite: Playing
outside

Mountain Biking, Crested Butte

Floyd Sedunov
Crested Butte
Community School
8 years old
Favorite: Biking

Ouray

Austin Cook
Telluride
Intermediate School
9 years old
Favorite: Biking and
climbing

Telluride

Annabelle Starr
Telluride
Intermediate School
10 years old
Favorite: Swimming
and reading

Mesa Verde

Jake Drever
Zealous School
13 years old
Favorite: Trail running

Four Corners

Haley Roberts
Crested Butte
Community School
10 years old
Favorite: Going to
Blue Mesa

Steam Train, Durango

Ava Tuitele
Flatirons
Elementary School
11 years old
Favorite: Biking and
swimming

Gator Reptile Park

Charlotte Newlun
West Jefferson
Middle School
13 years old
Favorite: Beach
volleyball

Great Sand Dunes

Davis Cameron
Miller Middle School
13 years old
Favorite: Camping

Ropes Course, Salida

Ryder Noakes
Eagle Valley Elementary
10 years old
Favorite: Swimming

Ghost Town

Amelie Derbomez
Willow Creek
Elementary School
11 years old
Favorite: Traveling,
exploring nature

Rafting, Buena Vista

Damaris Huffaker
Boulder High School
17 years old
Favorite: Watching the
sun rise

Collegiate Peaks

Devyn Grundy
Monte Vista
On-line Academy
16 years old
Favorite: Hiking

Cowboys

Hazel Nall
Eagle Valley
High School
14 years old
Favorite: Hiking

Royal Gorge

Ilo Hawley
Crested Butte
Elementary School
10 years old
Favorite: Smelling
flowers and biking

State Fair, Pueblo

Sophia Ammann
Boulder High School
14 years old
Favorite: Hike with
dogs

Pikes Peak

Aarna Dhawan
Willow Creek
Elementary School
9 years old
Favorite: Having lots
of fun!

Garden of the Gods, Colorado Springs

Evan Lee
Willow Creek
Elementary School
11 years old
Favorite: Traveling
and playing soccer

Red Rocks

Boston Suarez
Home Schooled
12 years old
Favorite: Drawing

Rockies Baseball, Denver

Tristan Llado
Willow Creek
Elementary School
11 years old
Favorite: Hanging out
with friends

Your Colorado Adventure

Roy Wang
Willow Creek
Elementary School
10 years old
Favorite: Playing
with friends

ZiPlining

SteamBoat SPrings

Rocky Mountain National Park

Grand Lake

VAIL

Winter Park

EaGLE

Colorado National Monument

WOODWARD

ASPEN

LAKE DILLON

HOT SPRINGS

BRECKENRIDGE

Buena Vista

14ers

CRESTED BUTTE

Telluride

OURAY

St. Elmo Ghost Town

Salida

Mesa Verde

Colorado CowBoys

Great Sand Dunes

Four Corners

Durango

Fort Collins

Boulder

RED ROCKS

Colorado Rockies Baseball

Garden of the GODS

Pikes Peak

Royal Gorge

Colorado State Fair

Rodeo

Colorado Gators Reptile Park

WELCOME TO COLORFUL COLORADO

"Wake up Mort!"

My stepmom, dad, li'l sis, Boo the Floppy Puppy, Mort the Moose, and I were ready to hit the road. Mort and I had packed our bikes, helmets, wetsuits, paddle boards and so much more. We had been to Colorado in the winter, but never in the summer.

We buckled our seat belts and away we went on our Colorado summer road trip adventure!

As we drove, Mort and I watched the sun blink-blink-blink through the trees and fell back asleep until we made it to our first stop, Boulder, Colorado.

First stop, breakfast in Boulder.

Boulder is famous for the Flatirons. The Flatirons are rocks that are taller than skyscrapers.

Dad had taught us that it was important to try new things. So for breakfast, we ate gigantic biscuits and funny shaped donuts called beignets.

After a few big bites, Mort and I were really full and ready for the next stop on our adventure.

Next stop, Fort Collins and Fort Fun.

As you can imagine, there were lots of fun things to do at Fort Fun. But of course, our favorite thing was to launch water balloons from their water balloon launcher.

Then, instead of balloons, I decided to try launching Mort. He didn't think that was so funny though.

Next stop, hiking in Rocky Mountain National Park.

While at the park we hiked the Wild Basin Trifecta. Well, I hiked and Mort took a ride in my backpack.

We saw Copeland Falls, Ouzel Falls and Calypso Cascades.

I imagined Orca whales dancing in the falls. Mort tested the water with his hoof. It was cold!

Next stop, Grand Lake.

The next day we went paddle boarding in Grand Lake. Mort and I have skills so we weren't worried about the fact it was our first time.

As we squeezed into our wetsuits, I said to Mort, "One of the best things about being a Colorado kid is that you have a lot of AWESOME gear."

Feeling proud, Mort stood tall and posed for a selfie.

After paddle boarding, it was time to pack our things and get back on the road.

Mort and I passed the time by playing "I Spy," and every once in a while I bugged my li'l sis.

I said to Mort, "That's just what kids do on road trips." Mort joined in and made a funny face too while I watched the sun go down. The sky turned lavender, pink and blue.

Next stop, Steamboat Springs.

As we arrived in Steamboat Springs we couldn't believe our eyes. The Steamboat sky was dotted with giant, candy-colored balloons way up high.

Mort and I imagined floating from cloud to cloud in our own Colorado colored hot air balloon.

Mort smiled and took a deep breath of the cool, fresh air.

Lindsay C.

Next stop, the rodeo and mutton bustin'.

Mutton bustin' was like riding a horse, but instead of a horse, we were riding a sheep – something much more our size.

Mort and I are pretty strong, so riding the sheep for as long as we could wasn't a problem at all.

Next stop, Winter Park.

My Dad told us that there were many different types of biking in Colorado such as mountain, enduro, downhill and BMX biking. That was just for starters.

Mort and I wanted to try them all, but Trestle Park in Winter Park was known for EXTREME downhill mountain biking.

"Extreme? This is right up our alley," I said to Mort. Mort agreed. He liked anything EXTREME.

Next stop, Lake Dillon.

Lake Dillon is a reservoir that was created a long time ago to hold water for things like drinking and taking baths.

Mort and I skipped some stones and counted the number of skips the stones took on top of the water before they sunk out of sight.

"I hate baths," I said to Mort.

Mort didn't like baths much either.

Next stop, Breckenridge.

Since Mort and I like shopping about as much as we like taking baths, we decided to let my stepmom, li'l sis and my dad take the lead.

Instead of shopping, Mort and I jumped from rock to rock on the sidewalk.

"Don't touch the ground," I said to Mort, "or you will be eaten alive!"

Next stop, Woodward at Copper Mountain for some snowboarding in the summer.

Snowboarding in the summer? We weren't sure how that worked but Mort was "all in" and so was I.

While snowboarding in the sun, Mort caught huge air and a tan at the same time.

I said to Mort, "How do they keep the snow from melting in the sun?" Mort said, he wasn't sure, but it was a big "W" as far as he was concerned.

Next stop, Vail.

In Vail, it was time to catch a ride on the alpine coaster on the top of Vail mountain.

Alpine coasters are roller coasters but better because they start off at the top of a mountain.

Mort, me and my stepmom giggled and screamed the whole 3,400 feet down the mountain.

Next stop, Eagle.

On our way to Grand Junction, we decided to stop in Eagle to see an outdoor concert.

At the concert, Mort and I laid down in the grass, ate cheese and crackers and listened to the music.

I said to Boo, "It doesn't get much better than this."

Boo would have agreed but he was fast asleep.

Next stop, Grand Junction and Colorado National Monument.

My stepmom told us there were eight National Monuments in Colorado and Colorado National Monument was one of them.

Dinosaurs used to live here which made sense because the rocks were as tall or taller than dinosaurs.

Next stop, hot springs.

On our way to Aspen we stopped at the hot springs to do one of our favorite things, swim.

We learned that there are over 50 hot springs in Colorado. Some are even secret.

I said to Mort, "Next time we are in Colorado let's find a secret one." Mort loved secrets.

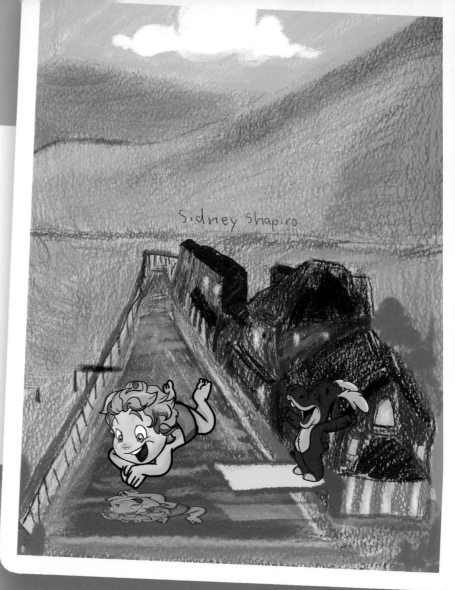

Sidney Shapiro

Next stop, Aspen.

The next morning Mort and I were ready to hit the horseback riding trail up to the Maroon Bells.

As we rode, my horse kept bending to sneak bites of grass which made my ankles bump into the Aspen trees. Sometimes I let her eat the grass and sometimes we had to keep going. That was just the way my horse and I worked it out.

Mort decided to eat some grass too.

Ana Jaramai

Next stop, Camping.

While we were camping, Mort, my li'l sis and I ate s'mores and made wishes on shooting stars while the smoke from the fire kept us on the move. Even Boo the Floppy Puppy joined in the fun.

I noticed my stepmom trying to keep track of us and the fire while we made more wishes and roasted more marshmallows.

My favorite Colorado camping experience:
_____
_____
_____
_____
_____
_____
_____
_____

Next stop, Crested Butte.

Time to ride the 401!

As we rode our bikes, the wildflowers on the 401 mountain bike trail clicked, twinkled and clicked against our handlebars making our clothes wet with dew.

Our skin got a little bit itchy from the wet flowers, but Mort and I didn't mind. The views took our minds off of the itch.

Next stop, Ouray.

Ouray is a western town that is surrounded by jagged mountains. The place has an ice cream shop and a candy store.

Our stepmom and dad let us order a double scoop.

As I ate I said to Mort, "If you added gummy goodness to this ice cream cone the taste would be life-changing."

Mort was too busy eating to say anything.

annabelle ★

Next stop, Telluride.

Telluride has the only public gondola transportation system in the world.

Mort, my li'l sis and I decided to ride the gondola around and again with my dad. If you looked down from the gondola you could sometimes see deer, elk and even a bear if you were lucky.

Next stop, Mesa Verde.

The Puebloans built houses under cliffs at Mesa Verde.

As it turned out, no one knew why they decided to build their houses there.

When we got back to our campsite, Mort and I tried building a fort from rocks and sand like the Puebloans.

I said to Mort, "This fort is pretty decent for a boy and a moose." Mort thought so too.

Haley Roberts

Next stop, Four Corners Monument.

Four Corners Monument is the place where the four corners of Colorado, Utah, Arizona, and New Mexico meet.

Mort and I decided to do some push-ups with one hand in Utah, the other in Colorado, and our feet in Arizona and New Mexico.

That night I asked Mort what his favorite part of the trip was so far. Mort said he couldn't decide.

Mort licked his lips thinking of breakfast the next morning as we both fell fast asleep under the stars.

Next Stop, Durango.

In Durango we rode the steam engine train on the narrow gauge railroad. My dad told us that in the 1800's thousands of people came to Colorado by train to mine for silver and gold.

As we watched out the window, we noticed the mountains were so tall that a cloud got stuck against one of them.

Next stop, a park full of gators.

When I thought of Colorado I didn't think of alligators. I was sure that gators were more of a Florida thing. But to our surprise, dad noticed a sign that said, "Colorado Gators Reptile Park."

When we arrived at the park, dad gave us his change to get some special gator chow to feed the gators. Mort didn't want to get too close, so he gave his chow to me.

"Thanks, Mort," I said. Mort said, "No. Really, thank you."

Next stop, Great Sand Dunes National Park.

At the park, my li'l sis, Mort and I ran up the sand dunes. Then we slid down on our snowboards. And then we ran up again.

You could roll, slide, jump and tumble all day, and never get hurt. It was sand.

Mort discovered that when you slide on the sand—like you are sliding into first base—you make a funny fart sound.

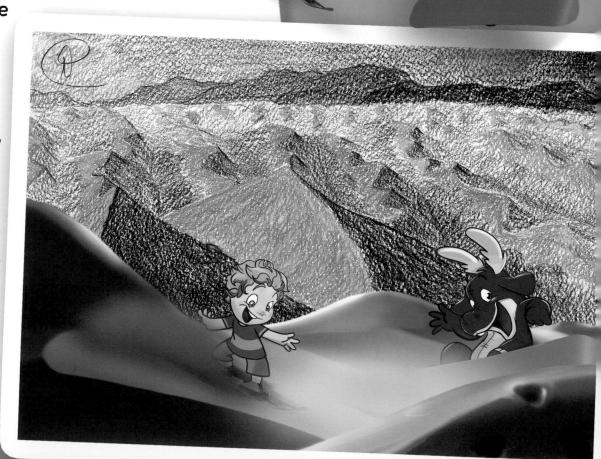

Next stop, Salida.

It was time for the ropes course and ziplining in Salida.

When you zipline you are strapped into a harness and then you fly through the sky really fast.

"Hold on Mort!" I said as we zinged across the Canyon.

Mort yelled, "Yahoo!"

Next stop, Saint Elmo Ghost Town.

I have to admit I was a little nervous about our next stop.....a ghost town.

My li'l sis told us that ghost towns are just towns where people used to live. There aren't really any ghosts there.

Mort and I said we believed her, but we were sure we saw at least one or two ghosts.

Next stop, Buena Vista.

Now it was time to hit the water and go whitewater rafting.

Mort and I decided to sit at the front of the raft which is called riding rodeo. Of course, this is where you got the wettest.

We both howled "Whoo-hoo!" as the waves washed over us and into the raft.

Mort and I were soaked.

Next stop, Collegiate Peaks.

As we drove from Buena Vista to the Royal Gorge we stopped to look at the Collegiate Peaks.

The Collegiate Peaks are some of the highest fourteeners in Colorado, and are named after famous universities.

A 14er is a mountain that is over fourteen thousand feet tall.

Mort and I had a hard time imagining fourteen thousand feet. But looking at Harvard Peak we knew that it was seriously high.

My dad told us Colorado has fifty-eight 14ers in total.

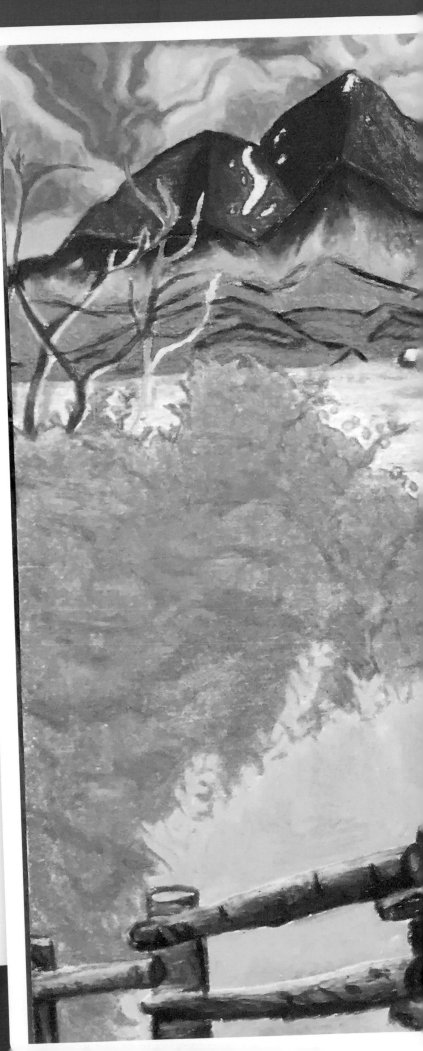

Colorado is famous for its cowboys.

Cowboys drove cattle across the wild frontier and slept under the stars.

Their trusty horses took them over mountains and across rivers.

You can spot a cowboy in Colorado because they are usually wearing a cowboy hat and cowboy boots.

Next stop, Royal Gorge.

The Gorge was 1250 feet deep, which I told Mort was almost the same as a 115-story skyscraper.

This fact made Mort feel sick in a good way about our next adventure, flying over the Royal Gorge in a giant swing!

Mort pulled the release cord and zoom! We screamed as loud as we could and felt our stomachs drop to the bottom of the Gorge.

Next stop, the Colorado State Fair.

At the State Fair, my dad and stepmom rode the Ferris wheel while we ate cotton candy and played games.

Mort liked the basketball shot and I liked throwing darts at the balloons.

Next stop, Pikes Peak.

Mort and I were about to summit our first fourteener—in a car.

As we drove to the top of Pikes Peak, Mort and I kept looking over the edge of the road to make ourselves feel queasy. We told our stepmom it was just for fun.

So we didn't get completely sick, we took breaks by looking out the window the other way .

Next Stop, Colorado Springs and Garden of the Gods.

Mort and my li'l sis imagined Garden of the Gods must be filled with rainbow-colored flowers.

When we got there we saw it was much better than just a garden because it had towering rocks that you could climb on.

Next stop, Red Rocks Amphitheatre.

Red Rocks is an outdoor amphitheatre created by rocks bigger then you could ever dream of. My dad said that it was "acoustically" perfect.

Mort and I had no idea what that meant.

I said to Mort, "This gives a whole new meaning to a ROCK and roll concert."

Mort wiggled and giggled at my joke.

Last stop, Denver.

For our final stop, Mort, my li'l sis and I got to watch the Colorado Rockies game. We sang "Take Me Out To The Ball Game," ate hot dogs, watched the game and wished we had one more stop left.

The game was the perfect ending to our EPIC Colorado summer road trip adventure.

Put your favorite
Colorado adventure
photo here.

Write about your favorite
Colorado adventure!

Thank you for reading
Eli and Mort's Epic Adventures
Colorado Summer Road Trip.

Check out Eli and Mort's other epic adventures.

Follow Eli and Mort!

www.eliandmort.com   facebook.com/eliandmort   instagram.com/eliandmort